ISBN 0-89659-175-1

THE FOREIGN LEGION

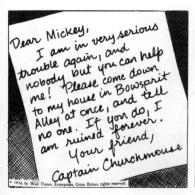

SO MICKEY HAS FINISHED HIS STINT IN THE FOREIGN LEGION! HE SOON REACHES THE PORT OF AITA KLAH KURFU AND TAKES "TRIGGER" HAWKES ABOARD SHIP!

FINALLY, AFTER A RESTFUL AND UNEVENTFUL VOYAGE, MICKEY'S SHIP DOCKS AT HOME! AND, AS HE WALKS DOWN THE GANG-PLANK—